For Mark and Sarah,

whose playfulness inspired the writing of this book.

I love our little family! –J.C.N.

For Saha, who is always spunky. –S.S.

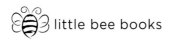

little bee books

An imprint of Bonnier Publishing USA
251 Park Avenue South, New York, NY 10010
Text copyright © 2017 by Judy Carey Nevin
Illustrations copyright © 2017 by Stephanie Six
All rights reserved, including the right of reproduction in whole or in part in
any form. LITTLE BEE BOOKS is a trademark of Bonnier Publishing USA,
and associated colophon is a trademark of Bonnier Publishing USA.
Manufactured in China LEO 0117
First Edition 10 9 8 7 6 5 4 3 2 1
ISBN 978-1-4998-0197-2
littlebeebooks.com
bonnierpublishingusa.com

Library of Congress Cataloging-in-Publication Data
Names: Nevin, Judy Carey, author. | Six, Stephanie, illustrator.
Title: What Daddies Like / by Judy Carey Nevin ; illustrated by Stephanie Six.
Description: New York : Little Bee Books, [2017] | Summary: Illustrations and simple text
reveal what fathers like through how they play with their babies.
Identifiers: LCCN 2015049774 | ISBN 9781499801972 (hardcover)
Subjects: | CYAC: Fathers—Fiction. | Babies—Fiction. | Parent and child—Fiction.
Classification: LCC PZ7.1.N485 Wh 2017 | DDC [E]—dc23
LC record available at https://lccn.loc.gov/2015049774

What Daddies Like

by Judy Carey Nevin

illustrated by Stephanie Six

 little bee books

Daddies like smooches.

Daddies like hugs.

Daddies like "Good morning to you!"

Daddies like adventures.

Daddies like swings.

Daddies

like

playing

kangaroo.

Daddies like monsters.

Daddies like roars.

Daddies like quiet time, too.

Daddies like splashes.

Daddies like boats.

Daddies like peekaboo.

Daddies like jammies.

Daddies like stars.

Daddies like night-lights, it's true.

Daddies like snuggles.

Daddies like sleep.

And most of all...

Daddies like
"I love you!"